Put Beginning Readers on the Right Track with
ALL ABOARD READING™

The All Aboard Reading series is especially for beginning readers. Written by noted authors and illustrated in full color, these are books that children really and truly *want* to read—books to excite their imagination, tickle their funny bone, expand their interests, and support their feelings. With three different reading levels, All Aboard Reading lets you choose which books are most appropriate for your children and their growing abilities.

Level 1—for Preschool through First Grade Children
Level 1 books have very few lines per page, very large type, easy words, lots of repetition, and pictures with visual "cues" to help children figure out the words on the page.

Level 2—for First Grade to Third Grade Children
Level 2 books are printed in slightly smaller type than Level 1 books. The stories are more complex but there is still lots of repetition in the text and many pictures. The sentences are quite simple and are broken up into short lines to make reading easier.

Level 3—for Second through Third Grade Children
Level 3 books have considerably longer texts, use harder words and more complicated sentences.

All Aboard for happy reading!

For Susan's big sister,
Carolyn Hosley.

Library of Congress Cataloging-in-Publication Data
Buller, Jon, 1943–   Mike and the magic cookies / by Jon Buller and Susan Schade.   p.   cm.
—(All aboard reading) Summary: Mike's trip to the store for animal cookies results in magical changes in each member of his family.   [1. Magic—Fiction.   2. Cookies—Fiction.
3. Animals—Fiction.] I. Schade, Susan.   II. Title.   III. Series. PZ7.B9135Mi
1992 [E]—dc20 91-33960   CIP   AC

ISBN 0-448-40388-9 (GB)   A B C D E F G H I J
ISBN 0-448-40386-2 (pbk.)   A B C D E F G H I J

ALL
ABOARD
READING™

Level 3
Grades 2-3

MIKE AND THE

MAGIC COOKIES

By Jon Buller and Susan Schade

Grosset & Dunlap • New York

This is our cat, Ducky.

She has no tail, and she likes to
go swimming.

But that's not all.

She is LIVING PROOF that I, Mike
Tracy, battled the forces of evil in the
dark forest—and won!

It was last summer.
All of my friends were at camp.

I was up in my tree house reading
my comics. But even "Super Hunk" was
getting boring. Everything was getting
boring.

And I was really getting sick of Tracy
family cookouts!

I could see everyone down in the
backyard.

My father was starting up the grill.

My mother was chasing one of the
ducks with a broom.

That duck was a real pest. Whenever
we had a cookout, it would come up
from the pond and try to steal our food.

My sister, Rose, was playing with her
stupid dolls, Kim and Barney. They were
getting married for the one millionth
time. I could hear her singing "Here
Comes the Bride." Pretty sick.

"Mike!" my mother called up to me. "We don't have anything for dessert. Will you ride down to the Stop and Spend and get some cookies?"

"All right," I said with a sigh. I was even sick of riding my bike.

Mom gave me some money.

I got on my Super Hunk bike. I decided to take the shortcut through the woods.

"Who knows what evil lurks in the heart of the forest?" I cried as I rode off.

That was a joke. Ha, ha. Not very funny, as it turned out.

I was riding fast.

I went over a little bridge by a waterfall.

That was strange. I didn't remember a little bridge. Or a waterfall.

In fact, everything looked different. Sort of dark...and spooky.

"I must be lost," I said to myself.

But the path was wide and clear. It even seemed to open up in front of me as I rode along.

All at once I smelled something. Something good! The smell seemed to be pulling me down the path, farther and farther into the dark forest.

Then I saw a little bake shop. A man wearing an apron was watching me from the door.

"I think I am lost," I called. "Is this the way to the store?"

"This is the store!" he said. "What do you need?"

I hesitated. It wasn't the store we usually go to.

"Hurry up!" he said. "I haven't got all day."

I left my bike against a tree. "I need some cookies," I said.

"Aha!" he cried. "I have just the thing. Freshly baked animal cookies!" And he pulled me into the shop.

The inside of the shop was amazing!
My mouth started watering.

"Can't make up your mind?" The
man laughed. "Let me help you." And
he snapped open a little white bag.

16

"A rabbit for Mike," he said to himself. "A pig for Rose, a chicken for Mrs. Tracy, and a nice frog for Mr. Tracy."

The smell of the cookies was driving me crazy. I didn't even wonder how he knew our names!

"Twenty-five cents each," the man said. "That will be one dollar."

I gave him my dollar. He handed me
the bag. Then he skipped out and held
the door open for me.

I hung back a little. The smell made
me greedy. And I still had two quarters.

Quickly I grabbed two more cookies—
a cat and a gorilla. I put the money on
the counter.

I followed the man out.

"Have a nice day," he said to me, grinning.

When I got home, everyone was waiting.

"Look at these great cookies," I said. "They come from a new store." I took the cookies out and put them on a plate. There was the pig, the chicken, the frog, the rabbit, the gorilla, and the cat.

Rose and my mother and my father all stared at the cookies. Their eyes got big and round. Dad licked his lips.

Rose grabbed the pig cookie. She popped the whole thing into her mouth.

My mother didn't say a word about waiting for dessert. She just picked up the chicken cookie, took a big bite, closed her eyes, and smiled.

My father took the frog cookie. He went off toward the pond, munching.

That left the rabbit, the cat, and the gorilla. It almost seemed as if the rabbit cookie had my name on it. So I ate it.

I didn't feel much like climbing up to my tree house. I sat down on the grass.

Sniff, sniff. The air was full of new smells. Sniff, sniff, sniff. It made my nose twitch.

I put my nose down to sniff the grass. Then I started eating it. "This is really strange," I thought. "I must be getting sick."

I looked at myself in the car mirror. My nose was getting pink. And my face was kind of pale. "I think I'll tell Mom I'm sick," I decided. I went to look for her.

I passed my sister, Rose. She was
lying in a mud puddle in her pink dress.
That wasn't like Rose at all. Clean is
her middle name.

"You better get out of there," I said.
"Dad is going to be really mad at you."

But Dad didn't seem to mind. He was
sitting at the edge of the pond in <u>his</u>
good clothes. He was making funny
noises.

Something strange <u>was</u> going on!

"Mom!" I called. There was no answer. Just a squawk from behind the house. Then I saw her. She had made a nest in the wheelbarrow. And she was sitting on it! She clucked at me and shooed me away.

Now I understood what was happening!

"Dad! Dad!" I cried. "We are all turning into animals. Just like the cookies we ate!"

"Ga-dunk!" said Dad. He stuck out his tongue to catch a fly.

I could see Dad wasn't going to be much help.

I didn't know what to do.

I stood very still. I listened and watched and sniffed the air. I tried to think. But it was hard! It felt like my brain was shrinking.

"The cookies must be magic," I finally decided. "So that means the baker must be a wizard! He has put us under a spell for some evil purpose!"

That was all the thinking I could do with my rabbit brain. I knew that only the wizard could break the spell.

I hopped a few hops down the path. Then I stopped and listened. The woods seemed full of danger. I stood very still. Nothing moved but my nose and whiskers.

Whiskers! Oh, no! There was no time to lose.

I ran the rest of the way.

I found the wizard. He was standing over a bubbling pot.

He looked happy to see me. "I knew you would be back!"

"If this is a joke," I squeaked, "I don't think it's very funny. My father is eating flies. And my mother looks like she is ready to lay an egg!"

The wizard just smiled. "And Rose?" he asked.

"She is rolling around in the mud!"

"Excellent, excellent!" he cried. "I love bacon. I love fried chicken. I love frog's legs. But, of course, my favorite is RABBIT STEW!"

And he reached out to grab me.

Luckily rabbits can run faster than wizards.

When I got home my little heart was thumping.

I looked around.

It was just as I had feared! Everyone was getting worse. Dad was turning green. Rose was growing fatter and fatter. And Mom was getting a beak!

What could I do? I didn't know any magic! How could a mere boy in a rabbit body stop an evil wizard?

I hopped on the table and stared at the two cookies that were left. The gorilla and the cat.

Hmmm. A gorilla.

I still had a big-enough brain to come up with an idea. I held the gorilla cookie in my paws and munched it down.

Right away I started to feel bigger and stronger.

BOOM! BOOM! BOOM! I pounded
on my chest.

"ARRUUUUGAH!"

I stormed through the woods. The
ground shook. Little animals ran and hid.

I came to the bake shop.

"OPEN UP!" I yelled.

There was no answer. So I kicked in the door.

I caught the wizard just as he was trying to sneak out the back door. "Not so fast!" I said.

"I never gave you a gorilla cookie!" he yelled. "How did you get one?"

"Never mind. Just give me some people cookies. And make them Tracys!"

"Phooey," said the wizard. He took a bowl of batter. He threw some pink powder into it. Fzzzt! Fzzzt! Then he spooned the batter into a pan. He made four cookies. A blob for each body. A blob for each head. Blobs for arms and legs.

When he took the cookies out of the
oven, I said, "Let's see them." I wasn't
sure he could be trusted.

He showed me the cookies. They
were Tracys all right.

I slapped a dollar on the counter and
ran home. BOOM! BOOM! BOOM!

Right away I gave everyone their Tracy cookie. Rose gobbled hers up. She almost got my fingers at the same time.

Dad wouldn't even look at his. I lifted him out of the pond. "No more flies until you eat this!" I yelled.

He ate it. But he looked mad. "You'll thank me for this one day!" I said.

Mom pecked away at hers. And I ate mine.

Soon we were all back to normal.

"I must have dozed off," my mother said. "I had the strangest dream. All about eggs!"

"That was no dream," I said. "You were turning into a chicken!" And I told them all about the evil wizard and the magic cookies.

They looked at me like I was crazy. "It sounds like MAKE-BELIEVE cookies to me," Dad said.

Then I remembered the last cookie.

"I can prove it!" I said, searching for the cat cookie. It had been right there on the table. I moved some plates and stuff. And then I saw it. At least I saw part of it.

"Oh, no!" I cried. "Somebody ate the cat cookie! And all that's left is the tail!"

"Come on, Mike. Stop this nonsense." My father took the tail and threw it on the fire. FZZZT! It made a fizzy, pink pop.

Just then I heard a quack.

"It's that greedy duck again," my
mother said.

But there was no duck. Just a white
cat with an orange nose and orange feet.
And no tail!

We all looked at the grill. The cookie tail was still fizzing a little. Then we looked at the cat.

"Oh, my stars," said my mother in a small voice. "Mike was right! The duck ate the cat cookie. All but the tail."

"Quack! Quack!" said the cat. Then she walked down to the pond and started swimming around.

Like I said, we call her Ducky.